DISCARD

THE DREA

classic-minedition

North American edition published 2019 by Michael Neugebauer Publishing Ltd. Hong Kong

Text and illustration copyright © 2006 Robert Ingpen
Rights arranged with "minedition" Rights and Licensing AG, Zurich, Switzerland.

Michael Neugebauer Publishing Ltd.,
Unit 28, 5/F, Metro Centre, Phase 2, No. 21 Lam Hing Street,
Kowloon Bay, Kowloon, Hong Kong. e-mail: info@minedition.com
This book was printed in May 2019 at L.Rex Printing Co Ltd
3/F., Blue Box Factory Building, 25 Hing Wo Street, Tin Wan, Aberdeen, Hong Kong, China
Typesetting in der Alexa
Library of Congress Cataloging-in-Publication Data available upon request.

ISBN 978-988-8341-93-1
10 9 8 7 6 5 4 3 2 1
First Impression

For more information please visit our website: www.minedition.com

KEEPER

A letter to
Alice Elisabeth
from her grandfather,
Robert Ingpen

classic-min dition

Dear Alice –

This is a story about a man who collects dreams and keeps them safe. He is called The Dreamkeeper.

Nobody I know has ever seen him. We can only imagine what he looks like, although we do know a few things about him ...

We know he wears strange clothes which belong to earlier times, so he is probably quite old. He has charms and lures, all sewn or pinned or tied to his coat. In his pockets he keeps sweets and sours, and pieces of paper with messages on them.

Over his shoulder he carries a long bamboo pole with strange markings, which he uses to carry cages and traps he needs for collecting the dream creatures he finds. Sometimes he plays the bamboo pole as a flute. On his head he always wears an old stovepipe hat.

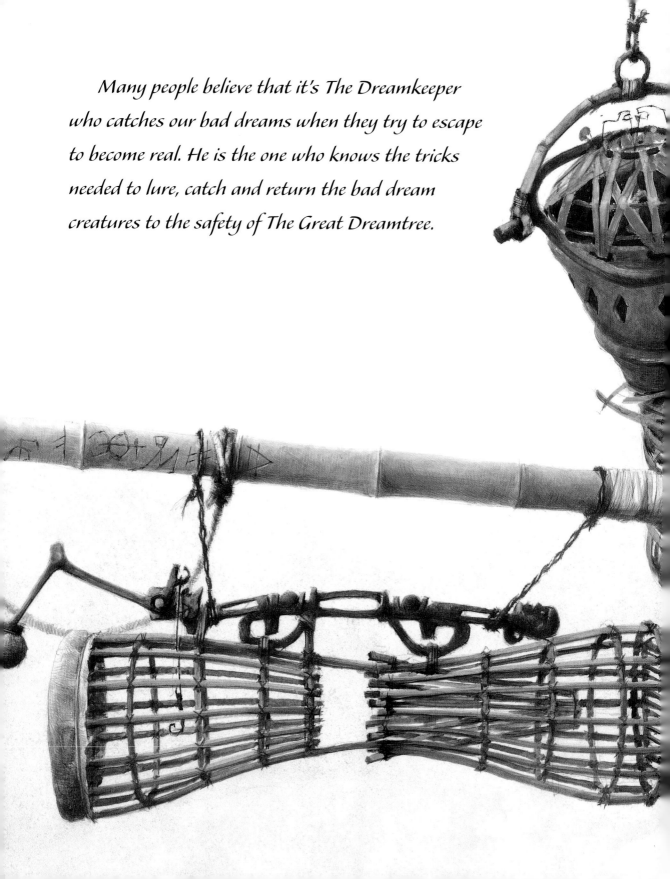

Many people believe that it's The Dreamkeeper who catches our bad dreams when they try to escape to become real. He is the one who knows the tricks needed to lure, catch and return the bad dream creatures to the safety of The Great Dreamtree.

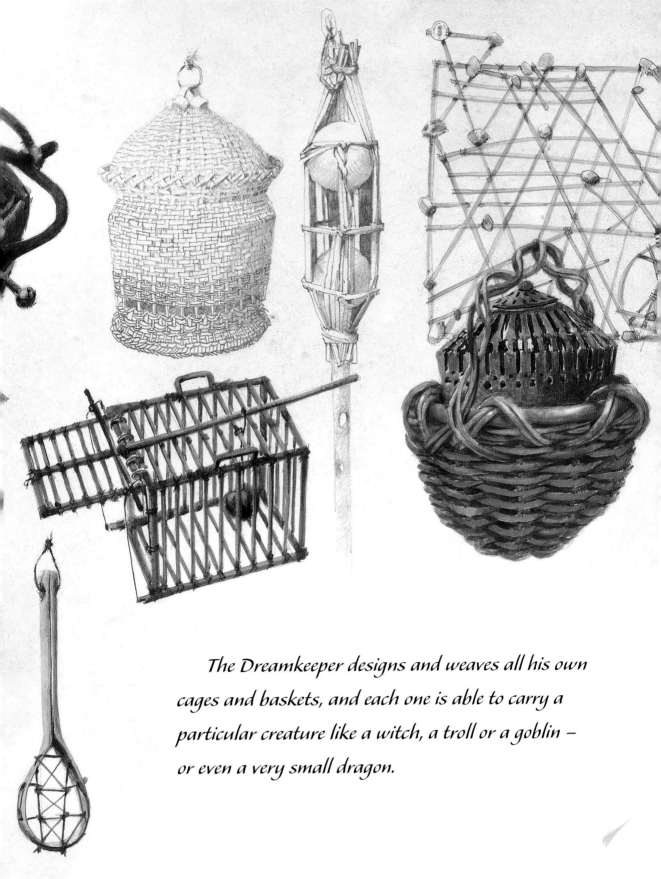

The Dreamkeeper designs and weaves all his own cages and baskets, and each one is able to carry a particular creature like a witch, a troll or a goblin – or even a very small dragon.

Dragons are difficult to catch. They are larger than almost any creature you can dream about, and more dangerous.

When he catches dragons, The Dreamkeeper quickly shrinks them with a mild reducing potion made from the juice of houseflies.

Once this is done they can be carried in a sling, since they are often still too large for baskets.

Witches are also quite hard to catch.
With the help of an ancient recipe,
The Dreamkeeper prepares a powerful
cocktail of bad-smelling herbs to make
his job easier.

With each full moon some witches try to sneak away from the coven to make mischief in reality. To stop them, The Dreamkeeper sets up an elderwood tripod on the route usually taken by loose witches. A dish is balanced on the tripod, and the herb mixture is lit and allowed to burn. The fumes will turn any witch into a raven for a short time. And ravens are easy to catch.

The recipe for the witch herb brew was invented by The Dreamkeeper's sister. She lives and works far away in an old pigeonhouse on stilts somewhere in the south of France. She works in her kitchen laboratory to keep her brother supplied with dream-catching aids, like magic sweets and sours, and of course her famous potion of Belief Syrup.

For centuries pigeons have lived in pigeonhouses, and they still do. People think they are kept there to be hunted, or to make droppings in order to fertilize the surrounding vineyards. But they really carry messages for The College of Great Belief which has its offices in this building. The president of the College is The Dreamkeeper, and when he is not traveling he lives there with his sister and a useful goblin called Tally.

There are many pigeonhouses in rural France, particularly in the south, and nobody knows exactly which is the one where the College operates. Perhaps the offices move from one to another so that we humans remain confused.

The College of Great Belief operates for the well-being of storybook characters, and sometimes for real people who appear in stories.

Although we do not know who is on the Council of the College, we do know that Tally is the Council Secretary. He runs the day-to-day affairs of the College when he is not out dream-catching with his master.

Inside the pigeonhouse Tally has a small room with a bed for sleeping, a box for keeping, and a desk for recording and reporting.

The room has two doors: one that leads to the kitchen where Belief Syrup and other magic potions are made, and another that leads to the library and meeting chamber where The Dreamkeeper bunks down when he needs to sleep. A small window high in the room leads to the wider world outside.

Until recently people
believed that The Dreamkeeper
worked alone and had no helpers.

This is not so; Tally is with
him at all times unless he is
contracted to do special projects
for other council members.
He keeps a tally of all The Dreamkeeper's
tricks, captures and conquests.

He has a memory as long as his
white beard, which he has to tuck into
his belt to stop tripping over himself.
Once he used to carry a sword to
cut up his food and defend himself,
but now he makes do with his ingenious
belief-powered remote control.

Goblins, elves, imps, gnomes and trolls are members of a family generally devoted to interrupting peaceful dreams.

They regularly escape the safety of The Great Dreamtree to upset the peace and quiet of humans. For example, they can make themselves invisible to most boys and girls, and certainly to all grown-ups.

The Dreamkeeper uses Tally, a tamed goblin, to make sure you will only imagine that you can see them. With his specially designed remote control Tally can expose the presence of any tricky goblin or hairy troll. Once they are no longer invisible it is easy for The Dreamkeeper to lure them into his baskets with colorful licorice devised by his clever sister.

Under the protection of the many branches of
The Great Dreamtree, good and evil spirits dwell
in harmony with the creatures of dreams.

The Dreamkeeper knows that spirits, like
ghosts, have a shape but no body, and that only
bad spirits cast shadows. The scary shadows
you see on the wall or ceiling at night often mark
the presence of an escaped bad spirit up to no
good. The Dreamkeeper has memorized the right
words and songs to persuade these spirits to
behave themselves and return.

When he speaks his voice is as soft as moss,
and his words as gentle as a falling feather. He
plays beautiful music on his long bamboo flute
to lure and seduce runaway spirits back to the
fabulous Great Dreamtree...

Now, Alice, I expect you have been waiting to hear how The Dreamkeeper catches and carries The Fairies. Well, I have a surprise for you; he doesn't. He couldn't even if he wanted to, because The Fairies, like shadows, cannot be caught. They are free to come and go whenever, however and wherever they like, forever.

You see, The Fairies do
not live within the branches
and roots of The Great Dreamtree.
They dwell inside hollow hills or
great mounds of earth built by
prehistoric tribes, either as forts
or monuments to past heroes.
Humans are advised to avoid these
places, especially after dark.
However, like most dream creatures,
The Fairies must come to The Great
Dreamtree to die. That is probably
why you never find fairy rings in
the garden.

So now you know about The Dreamkeeper.

He will never be far away when your mind is

somewhere between what is really happening

and what you imagine might happen.

    He lives in a world just around the corner

of your mind, where reality is an intruder and

dreams, both good and bad, come true.

And that's where you may find him and Tally.

    Safe traveling, good dreaming, and God bless,

Grandpa